baby bear sees
BLUE

ASHLEY WOLFF

SCHOLASTIC INC.

Deep down in the den,
Baby Bear wakes up.
He yawns and blinks
and stretches his stubby legs.

In the den's dark wall,
an opening slowly fills with light.
A glow creeps in.
"Who is warming me, Mama?"
asks Baby Bear.
"That is the sun," Mama says.

Baby Bear sees yellow.

At the mouth of the den,
leaves dance on a twig.
"Who is waving to me, Mama?"
asks Baby Bear.
"That is the oak," Mama says.

Baby Bear sees green.

High in the oak, a bird calls out.
Another bird answers.
"Who is singing to me, Mama?"
asks Baby Bear.
"Those are the jays," Mama says.

Baby Bear sees blue.

Mama Bear wades the swift river.
Baby Bear follows.
Suddenly a fish leaps!

"Mama! Who splashed me?"
asks Baby Bear.
"That is the trout," Mama says.

Baby Bear sees brown.

Mama and Baby climb into the meadow.
Baby Bear sniffs.

"What smells so good, Mama?"
asks Baby Bear.
"Those are the strawberries,"
Mama says.

Baby Bear sees red.

Mama Bear rests in the grass
while Baby Bear explores.
Bright wings flutter by.

"Who tickled me, Mama?"
asks Baby Bear.
"That is a butterfly,"
Mama says.

Baby Bear sees orange.

Baby Bear hears a deep rumble.
"Mama! Who is growling at me?"
"That is the thunder," Mama says.
"Let's hurry home!"

Baby Bear sees gray.

When the boom and grumble
move off down the valley,
Baby Bear peeks outside.
"Mama, look!"

"That is the rainbow," Mama says.

Mama and Baby curl together.
Baby Bear yawns.
"Good night, Baby Bear," Mama says.
"Good night, Mama," says Baby Bear.

Then Baby Bear closes his eyes
and sees nothing
but deep, soft black.

For Deane, my Mama Bear.
You showed me that beauty is everywhere.

ISBN 978-0-545-61216-6

12 11 10 9 8 7 6 5 4 3 2 1   14 15 16 17 18 19/0

Printed in the U.S.A.   08

This edition first printing, January 2014

Book design by Lauren Rille
The text for this book is set in Joppa.
The illustrations in this book are made by printing linoleum blocks in black on Arches Cover paper. These are then hand colored with watercolor.